WATCH OUT!
BIG BRO'S
COMING!

Jez Alborough

CANDLEWICK PRESS
CAMBRIDGE, MASSACHUSETTS

"Help!" squeaked a mouse.
   "He's coming!"

"Who's coming?" asked a frog.

"Big Bro," said the mouse.
   "He's rough, he's tough, and he's big."

"Big?" said the frog. "How big?"

The mouse stretched out his arms
   as wide as they could go.

"This big," he cried,
and he scampered off to hide.

"Look out!" croaked the frog.
    "Big Bro's coming!"

"Big who?" asked the parrot.

"Big Bro," said the frog. "He's rough,
    he's tough, and he's really big."

"Really big?" said the parrot. "How big?"

The frog
stretched out his arms
as wide as they could go.
"This big," he cried,
    and he hopped off
        to hide.

"Watch out!" squawked the parrot.
"Big Bro's coming!"

"Who's he?"
asked the chimpanzee.

"Don't you know Big Bro?"
asked the parrot. "He's rough,
he's tough, and he's ever so big."

"Ever so big?" said the chimpanzee.
"How big?"

The parrot stretched out his wings
as wide as they could go.
"This big," he cried,
and he flapped off
to hide.

"Ooh-ooh! Look out!"
whooped the chimpanzee.
"Big Bro's coming!"

"Big Joe?" said the elephant.

"No," said the chimpanzee. "Big Bro.
He's rough, he's tough, and everybody
knows how big Big Bro is."

The elephant shook his head.
"I don't," he said.

The chimpanzee stretched out his arms as wide as they could go. "This big," he cried.

"That big?" gulped the elephant. "Let's hide!"

So there they all were, hiding
and waiting, waiting and hiding.

"Where is he?"
asked the elephant.

"Shhh," said the chimpanzee.
"I don't know."

"Why don't you creep out
and take a look around?"
whispered the elephant.

"Not me,"
  said the chimpanzee.

"Not me,"
  said the parrot.

"Not me,"
  said the frog.

"All right," said the mouse.
  "Since you're all so
  frightened, I'll go."

The mouse tiptoed out from his hiding place ever so slowly.

He looked this way and that way to see if he could see Big Bro.

And then . . .
    "He's coming!"
shrieked
    the mouse.

"H . . .
    h . . .
        h . . .
            hide!"

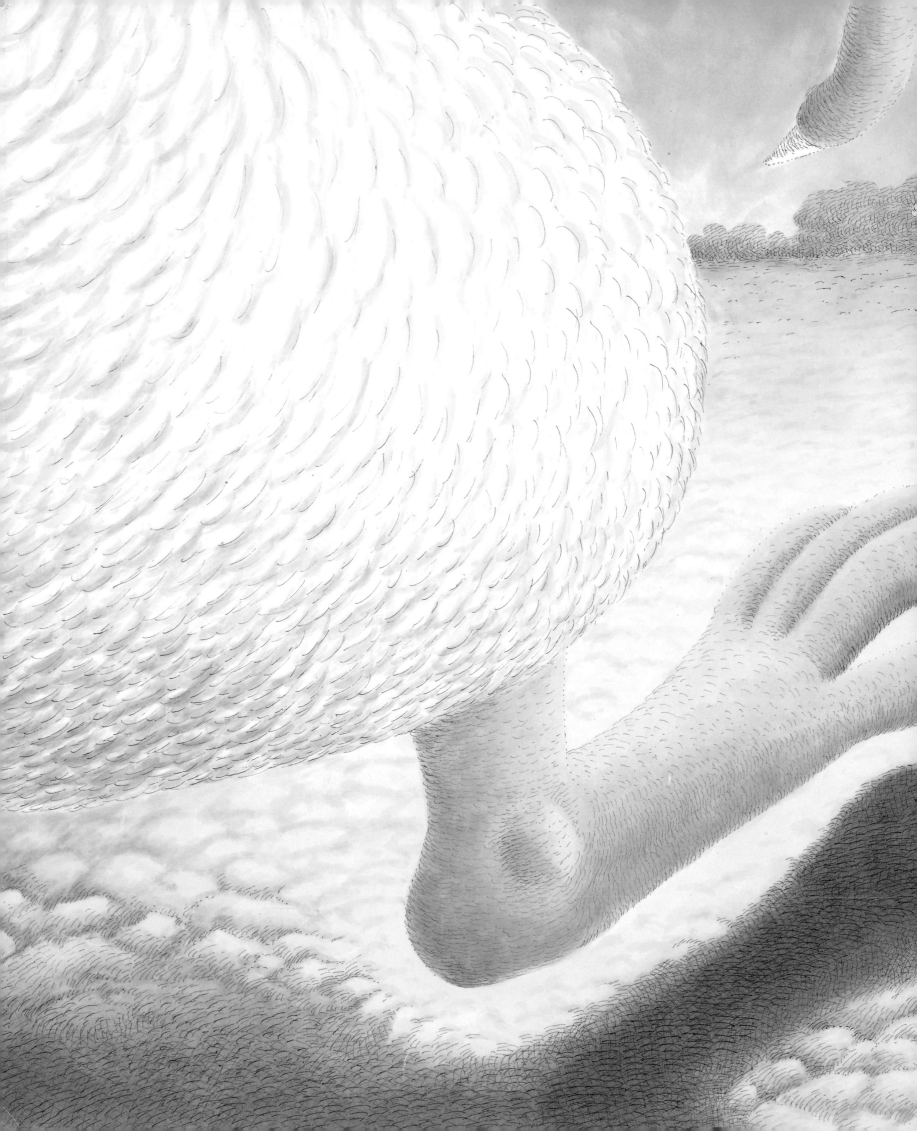

Big Bro came closer
and closer and closer.
They all covered their eyes.

"Oh, no," whispered the frog.

"Help," gasped the parrot.

"I can hear something coming,"
whined the chimpanzee.

"It's him," whimpered
the elephant.
"It's . . . it's . . ."

"BIG BRO!"

shrieked the mouse.

"Is that Big Bro?" asked the frog.

"He's tiny," said the parrot.

"Teeny-weeny," said the chimpanzee.

"He's a mouse," said the elephant.

Big Bro looked up at them all,
took a deep breath,
and said, . . .

"Come on, Little Bro," said Big Bro.
"Mom wants you back home *now*!"

"Wow," said the elephant.

"Phew," said the chimpanzee.

"He is rough," said the parrot.

"And tough," said the frog.

"Rough and tough," said Little Bro,
looking back over
his shoulder.

"And I *told* you
he was big!"